PAVEMENT PRAYERS

Ivan Arthur

En Route Books and Media, LLC
St. Louis, MO, USA

✹ENROUTE
Make the time

En Route Books and Media, LLC

5705 Rhodes Avenue

St. Louis, MO 63109

Cover credit: Sebastian Mahfood

ISBN-13: 978-1-956715-35-4

Library of Congress Control Number:

2022934048

Table of Contents

Dedicated to
the pavement dwellers of Mumbai
who inspired much of this book

Acknowledgements

It is to Ingrid, my wife to whom I went for insightful criticism after writing each chapter that this book owes much of its shape.

It was Mary Arthur, my mother, who taught me by rote most of the prayers that I have used here, though she may never recognize them in this book.

My father, Jossie, taught me the alternative approach to the folded hands.

Roxana and Ayesha gave silent support. Rohan gave me advice that often I did not follow; and he was proved right.

Lorna and Robin convinced me that this thing was worth publishing.

It was the late Frank Simoes, not I who made the first presentation of the manuscript to publishers. To me, Frank's support of the book meant a great deal. I will always remember the appreciation and encouragement he gave me when I needed it.

I thank Bishop Bosco for offering to write the Foreword and Walter Saldanha for casting his eagle eye over the text.

I am grateful to Fr. Erasto Fernandes for his help in getting the first edition of Pavement Prayers published and Sebastian Mahfood for his publication of the second edition.

Foreword

Pavement Prayers is a most unusual book and will be enjoyed, I believe, by all those who are ready to stray from the beaten literary track. In this book, Ivan Arthur makes us aware of a category of persons almost non-existent for the rest of society although they live in full view of the world – on the streets! To most of us, they are of no significance whatsoever and we pass them by as if they did not exist.

Pavement Prayers brings this group of people to life. As I read this book, I began to find them interesting as individuals as they emerged, one by one, each with his or her own personality. I came to know Gomti, Fat-fatia, Ganga, Neha, Purnima, Thambi, Savitri, Kalia, Mamta, Dondu and others. Gradually, I found them becoming my friends as I grew to like them and got interested in their joys and sufferings.

This book is written in the form of prayers – an outpouring of prayer from the hero John. No punction – no commas or full stops – just a torrent of sincere communication straight from the heart to the Lord, which has a striking beauty of its own.

For me personally, Ivan Arthur also raises religious questions in the course of the book. In answer to the unasked but implied question "Who is God?" we find that John, our pavement-hero-cum-artist, suffering practically from delirium, discovers God in his suffering:

"I do not know why my prayer to You is not the usual petition and self-pity and despair but just an unspoken but real sense of your presence somewhere amid the pain which at times looms so large that in that agonizing delirium I imagine it is You who are this Great Pain filling me and holding on to my being as if You do not want to let go"

To me the book asks questions about the way we pray. We are reminded in the preface about the inadequacy of the prayer book:

"...The Roman Catholic repertoire of prayer is impressive: rosaries, litanies, sequences, novenas, the missal, the breviary, the angelus, the daily family prayer book. These contain the magical words that the Church puts into the mouths of her faithful: pious, theologically sound, nice and neat formulae... But they are not John's words;

Philosophical speculation, religious reflection and theological challenges are to be found all through the narrative. Isn't faith a clinging to God in the midst of darkness? I saw it in John's fingering of the broken rosary beads in his pocket:

"I feel with thumb and forefinger the
metal figure of Him crucified on that little
cross of wood among the dirt and lint inside my trouser pocket giving shape in
that instant to the state of my personal
faith broken but there still . . . "

I am reminded too of the dangers of a religious practice focused on self:

"the perpetual petitions of the people for
cures from cancer and for jobs for husbands and for husbands for spinster
daughters."

Finally, as I came to the end of the book, I
began to find myself admiring the characters
more and more as courageous individuals
who could face tremendous difficulties and
sufferings with cheerfulness, optimism and
even joyful abandon; showing an "amazing
maturity of spirit, a serenity and near-
mystical outlook to life; evidence of a spirit
hammered into strength and resilience and
more: a spirit with more fiber than the flesh
and the intellect are heir to."

Ivan's writing is precise and incisive, deep and profound. What is more impressive is his humanity, warmth, kindness, friendliness, helpfulness, simplicity and humility – his personal charisma.

This book is not a "head" book. It does not deal with information, academics, scientific data or statistics, but it is a wonderful book for the heart in which one finds thoughtfulness, wisdom, insight, understanding, perspective, delight and meaning. It should also lead us to a deep sense of humility as we are reminded that while the world looks at the externals it is God who looks at the heart (1 Sam. 16,7). As Jesus said: "I tell you, the tax collectors and prostitutes are going to the Kingdom of God ahead of you" (Mt. 21, 31).

Bishop Bosco Penha,
Auxiliary Bishop,
Archdiocese of Mumbai

Preface

From one point of view, we can take this for what it seems to be: a story about the pavements of Mumbai and of a pavement dweller called John.

The Mumbai pavement is a paradox. This roofless expanse is for hundreds of thousands, a home that is in many ways kinder, more sustaining and more secure than the ones out of which they were driven. The very brutality of their relationships is their armor against uncertainty. Their lack of possessions is their wealth, because the whole city belongs to them. They have evolved their own rules of survival and indeed contentment, understanding the city as nobody else does; certainly better than the planners, the lawmakers and the administrators; knowing how to manipulate it to their advantage. They know what stirs the conscience of the rich, what moves the hearts of the middle-class and what loosens the grip of the law. They are the free people of the city, moving about wherever they want to. That is why thousands of families who have made their home on the pavements, never leave it, even after they have, by whatever means, managed to put by enough (and many of them do) to buy themselves a small abode in the suburbs (which they never do).

On the pavement near my office, I have seen three generations of families grow up over the years. The ones whom I saw as teenagers and snotty little urchins thirty years ago are

still there on that pavement, having celebrat-
ed marriages, births, and funerals at the same

roofless address. I have seen them grow gray,
wrinkled and obese; I have seen their infants
grow up and get married and they in turn
have had children. The pavement has taken
them to its bosom.

The pavement is wonderfully rich in story. For every twenty-or-so-steps that you take over it, your feet could be shuffling through chapters, or perhaps, volumes of intricate plot, moving human drama and the most thrilling narrative. More than any other institution, the pavement family is packed with incident -- unpredictable, challenging and continuous.

The following pages are my twenty-or-so steps of narrative, the story of John and his patch of pavement told in the most intimate form of narration: John's personal prayer.

This then, from another point of view, is a book of prayers that tell a story.

But of course, all prayers – all personal prayers– tell stories. They tell heroic tales of Herculean troubles surmounted, of miraculous escapes, of heart-wrenching tragedies and joyous endings, or they speak of simple lives of quiet existence. Prayer is, in many ways the spiritualization of incident, and in every fervent prayer one can find a short story or an epic sticking to it.

The story of John is a real one, though his character is fictitious. There are many Johns, if you care to spot them, on the pavements of Mumbai. My John has been put together out of the ones that I encountered.

I first met a kind of John when I was a child of four. With other four-year-olds, I was picking wild flowers on the side of the street opposite our home in Bandra, little white and yellow flowers that caught our fancy. We thought that they would look good on the altar. Just when we thought we had gathered enough, we heard someone moaning nearby and when we looked in the direction of the sound, we saw him. He was lying in the gutter that ran alongside the road.

"He's drunk," we said as we prepared to run. I was the slowest runner of the lot, which is why, as I struggled up from the steep slope, I heard him groan the words, "I'm not drunk. I'm hungry." I called my friends back and we bent down to look at him. He was decently dressed, down to his socks and shoes. He had a largish brown paper packet lying next to him. "I'm starving," he spoke in English, in a refined accent. "I need something to eat."

As luck would have it, a *puranpoli* woman was passing by, and she stopped, seeing us around this man in the gutter. She offered him a few puranpolis. In the meantime, I ran home and got him a glass of milk. After the puranpoli and milk had gone down, he opened the brown paper packet and showed us his drawings. He was an artist in search of a job.

Many years later, in the early sixties, I came across another variety of John: my father spoke to us of a brilliant young man in his office, a commercial artist of rare talent and wide reading. He wrote poetry and was an excellent illustrator. Unfortunately, like a few young people of that time, he got involved with the hippies of the day. Soon he gave up his job in favor of life with these people.

I was still studying for my graduation degree at that time, but years later, when I started work as a journalist, I noticed almost every day on the streets, a young man with a dirty satchel on his back. He looked as though he were high on something. Often I would see him with the hippies, looking as dirty as the city's beggars. Behind his wild, disheveled hair and beard, one noticed a sensitive pair of eyes. In my mind I linked him with the young artist of whom my father spoke, and more than once I almost went up to him to ask whether in fact he was the same person. I had visions of trying to rehabilitate the fellow, but I could never pick up enough courage to even get close to him. As time went by, he grew to look dirtier, leaner, wilder and more unfocussed. There were days when I saw children throw stones at him as they often do at mad people on the streets.

The pavements of Mumbai are full of people like these 'Johns', hundreds of men and women from respectable families who have drifted on to the streets or who have been thrust by circumstance into this strangely welcoming world of the footpath. My wife, Ingrid and I have had conversations with many of them and we have even become acquaintances of a few. Our friends are often surprised when these 'beggars' wave out to us like good friends as we walk past them. More than a couple of times we offered to try and put them into an institution that would take care of them, but they have always refused to be rehabilitated in any way. They are not prepared to trade the freedom of the streets for the relative comfort of a shelter.

From our individual encounters with these people we could not but note the stamp of the pavement on their spirit. The soul-crushing deprivation, cruelty and degradation of the streets had all but squeezed out all traces of spiritual energy in some, making them into either weak and indifferent floaters, waiting for the end, as it were, or into unconscionable agents of depravity, duplicity and crime. In a few others, however we witnessed an amazing maturity of spirit, a serenity and a near-mystical outlook to life; evidence of a sprit hammered into strength and resilience and more: a spirit with more fiber than the flesh and the intellect are heir to.

As housing for the spirit, the whorehouse and the monastery are neighbors here.

I made John a Christian, a Roman Catholic for my own literary convenience, to fit in with the design of the prayers. For one good reason: the Roman Catholic repertoire of prayer is impressive: rosaries, litanies, sequences, novenas, the missal, the breviary, the angelus, the daily family prayer book. These contain the magical words that the Church puts into the mouths of her faithful; pious, theologically sound, nice and neat formulae; prescribed telegraphic messages that we Johns can send to the Lord.

But they are not John's words; they will never express his particular feelings; they do not fit in with what he is going through at any moment. So, now and again, he has to put these fine prayer books aside and articulate what's in his mind and heart. His prayer then becomes different from that of the prayer books, or anything that was taught to him by priest or parent. Even though it expresses basically the same thought as that in the prayer book, it is different because the context, the relevance and the intensity of feeling are exclusively John's.

And the incoherence. Personal prayer can be
a messy affair. There you are, mind crowded
with compelling distractions, trying very hard
to talk to a God you cannot see; you are not
very sure that He is listening, and worse, you
are not sure that you are saying the right

things. Petition, studied praise, sanctimoni-
ousness, complaint, self-justification, self-
righteousness, self-pity, self-flagellation,
blame, bribery, quarrel, rationalization, all
these are the stuff of personal prayer. But
they are yours, they are sincere and they are
made of flesh and blood.

I have, scurrilously, if you will, translated the
nice, neat formulae of the Roman Catholic
prayer book into the messy, unpunctuated
incoherence of John, the pavement supplicant. Work, incident, location, thoughts, feelings, the twists and turns of his fate and the
various chapters in his lifetime have been
used as the altars before which the prayers
come unbidden. With the pavement as prayer
book and un unlikely John as our praying
protagonist, one may or may not find paral-
lels with one's own personal communion
with the Almighty, but then, on the other
hand, who knows, one just might!

Morning Prayer

Good morning my Lord I confess I didn't say my morning prayers like my mother had taught me to but it is not always a nice thing waking up on a pavement you know because you don't know what your wake-up call is going to be like though I've gone through them all or almost all for all these street-hardened years of dirty dawns oh yes I've felt the hard kick of a lazy boot that has blindly tripped on my sleeping body without so much as an apology and sometimes the hard kick of the boot of some

over-fed policeman with nothing better to do and at other times the furtive hand of an ap-

prentice pick-pocket getting a little cheap
practice on me and on some mornings the
warm trickle of that three-year-old's 5 am
relief or worse much worse and no excuses
Lord but I find it hard to make the sign of the
Cross on rudely awakened breast at those
times so will you hold it against me please tell
me will you hold it against me while today
ten minutes after my wake-up call and a slap-
dash wash at a burst water pipe I am crossing
the street on to the waterfront where early as
it is a few joggers are working at undoing the
venial sins of the belly and old men have
gathered to fill in the blanks of their generally
vacant days with at least some sunrise socia-
bility yes I see these early morning warm-ups
of the city's day and I marvel Lord at the
sense of discipline and purpose of people
who seem to have it all and I wonder if that is
why Lord you have given them that all or
have they got that all all by themselves without any help from you because they are so
smart and hard-working and such deserving

men and women I wonder as I stroll against a strong and refreshing breeze which quickly fills my lungs with goodness and I swallow gulps of this delicious nothingness as if it were going to run out on me ooh and ooh it

feels so good to know that it is the same qual-
ity of goodness that is being lavished on me
as on all these other motor car driven big
shot joggers and not all their money and influence can buy them anything more or better than what I am being given today thank
you thank you Lord and I ask myself in the
mindset of the street-set what would these big
shot joggers be willing to pay if you Lord
were selling this invigorating stuff by the cubic centimeter how much would they be willing to buy and would they haggle with you on
the price and would they try and beat you
down with their studied and much-practiced
negotiating skills I wonder because I am getting it free by the lungful and you can see it
has already cleared my head and scraped out
the phlegm from lungs and from my throat
yes and put a spring into my step and a smile
on my face and I notice a few joggers and
walkers looking at me as if I had no right to
look so contented and sprightly and one of
them slows down as he approaches from the

opposite side and stares at me and squints his
eye and as he passes me he turns around and
I turn around too getting a look at his face
while we continue in our own directions but
in that split second of a turned head my mind
does a flash-back to a face in an office of
many years ago which is the face of the walk-
er who walked by only now he doesn't quite
look like Pandu the peon he was then when I
knew him in nineteen-something-something
he was Pandu the tea boy the odd job boy the
naughty boy the cute fellow the everybody's
boy the anytime boy or the boy who would
do anything you wanted for a small tip
whether it be to fetch and carry or buy or fix
you could depend on Pandu the ever willing
and clever and resourceful yes Pandu would
get it for you be it a railway ticket during the
crowded season or a pornographic magazine
oh yes you could rely on Pandu the fellow
who everyone said would go far because he
was hard working and street smart and en-
terprising even then as a tea boy whose job

was only to distribute the tea for the pantry contractor Pandu would spend his own money and stock up on razor blades and chewing gum and batteries because he said these were the things that ran out without notice or even things like condoms and aphrodisiacs which the young bachelors felt embarrassed to ask for at the chemist's and that was all to the good so that Pandu could make a small profit on the side oh yes Pandu was a smart one and this is the same fellow I see today doing his morning walk in well-laundered shorts and tee-shirt and Nike jogging shoes looking every inch like one of the other big shot car owning joggers and I say to myself as he walks past me that morning that he hasn't recognized me because things have changed so much for him and a lot more for me with life having moved in wildly opposite directions and look how some people have climbed to higher and happier stations whilst I Lord I have come to this pavement and this day of tattered clothing and battered spirit and this

day of the uncertain wake-up call and wonder of wonders to this miraculous day when
in the sight of the whole world You in Your
divine power or is it playfulness have chosen
to tell me that I am equal to him and him and
her and all of them yahoo and alleluia my
spirit is laughing like a child inside me as I
now almost fly with arms outstretched and
fingers like palm leaves slicing the cool breeze
that sings joyful hosannas into my ears as I
run to the end of the waterfront where the sea
surrounds me on three sides and I face the
water for the while keeping the city behind
me with all its emotional excrement and the
foul breath of crime and inhumanity and op-
portunism and mindless urgency and before
long it does not exist for me I swear the city
has vanished completely and it is not there
for me oh no it is not there at all and Yesterday is swallowed up in the Now and I sense
this big presence of Is It You my Lord is it
You in that great big expanse of Youness between the canopy of blue above and the

dance of the waves below and I am lost in this
gust of this sacramental southwesterly that
has braced my spirit to feel that it is You of
my childhood catechism I see walking over
the waves coming from a distant shore and as
you come nearer I feel that my mind is playing tricks on me for I see you barefooted in
tattered jeans with a dirty satchel on your
back looking like another city vagrant in fact
quite like me with your hand outstretched
and beckoning me to take a step forward and
I say to myself that I have gone crazy and that
those substances I ingested years ago are even
now working on me for you would not even
if you chose to be incarnated today be part of
our pavement gang or would you I ask would
you walk with hand on shoulder with vaga-
bonds and pickpockets and pimps and prostitutes and beggars and would you sit with us
over a shared butt of a discarded cigarette to
listen to our tales of bravado of how one
outwitted the police and the other picked a
challenging pocket in broad daylight and yet

another got the better of that patch of slime
that tried to pay less for the sexual labors he
had come to hire from one of our pavement
sisters or would you share a meal of left-over
roti with the scum of the city oh would you
Lord would you I ask you and if you had to
do your last supper with us today what
would you use for bread and wine on our
pavement I wonder and in my glad delirium I
dare to think of all that mad divinity as a pos-
sibility within the fractured theology of the
moment as I reflect on how far this vessel
that is me has wandered from that shore for I
have let the waves toss me and the flying gulls
distract me and the winds blow me further
and further away and I close my eyes and lift
up my hands and I still see in the breeze that
runs through my hair and caresses my fingers
what looks to my happily delirious mind of
the moment like the hand of him who stilled
the waters and I sit down on a rock and I pick
up a stone and without looking up I scratch
upon another rock with all my strength the

image of that hand in my spirit's eye and then I continue sitting there for I don't know how long upon a rock facing the horizon looking out at the infinity of blankness inside of me and a nothingness outside me feeling weightless and infinitesimally tiny at one time and insubstantially huge at another till I am pulled out of my blankness by a warm sun that burns my neck and my shoulders but when I get up on my feet to leave I notice under the stone I used for etching my vision of the hand a folded piece of paper on which are scrawled a few words saying that the writer recognized me as John the brilliant illustrator of long time ago and that he recognized me from the drawing on the rock because no one else could draw fingers like John did and it was signed *Pandu* and I have not yet said my morning prayers or have I

Grace Before

Bless us O lord and these Thy gifts which from Thy bounty this rich city businessman has received in such plenty that we are able to eat from the basketfuls that were left over after he and his friends had finished their fork-and-knife pickings as you can see Lord Your multiplication of loaves and fishes still goes on in our modern times Oh yes I can picture those dainty morsels going into mouth-freshened cavities chewing slowly with decent jaw movements and clever talk morsels sliding down their healthy gullets into stomachs already full or half full or at least slightly full because you know how it is Lord you know that they cannot afford to put on kilograms or centimeters

because it is not quite the fashion these days
to look fat and in fact the more you possess
the thinner you should be and all that O Lord
bless us and these Thy gifts which I am about
to put into my mouth which has since the
morning accepted into it only gulps of water
from the street-side water fountains and the
comforting nicotine-rich fomentation of
those butts of half-smoked filter-tipped ciga-
rettes thrown by other rich city folk oh bless
them and thank You thank you Lord for all
those rich folk in the city as Dives would have
thanked you for Lazarus and his crumbs I
thank You thank You but now and again I
look at those well-pressed suits inside gleaming motor cars and I look at their faces and I
try and smuggle myself into their minds and I
can feel their feelings when some disfigured
limb in deliberately torn sleeve reaches out
with voice rehearsed to move wooden hearts
yes I have observed the struggle inside head
and heart to make that one small decision to
let that one small crumb of currency drop

from those limousine heights on to wrinkled
upturned palm below Oh that poor little rich

man who half an hour earlier with one stroke
of his Montblanc nib had signed over a million rupees and more to a name across the
globe and now poor rich man is thrown to

the two lions of Conscience and Judgment
who between them will have his peace of
mind mangled anyway so help him God yes
help him know if that wrinkled upturned paw
is genuine and not counterfeit stuff created
by some surgeon of the street in some nocturnal clandestine limb-sawing factory because if that is so he is afraid that he will be
sponsoring an industry bigger perhaps than
the one underneath his Montblanc nib and
the resulting damage will be big very big even
bigger than the damage that his Montblanc
nib on million-rupee cheque can do to his
enterprise because that crumb falling from
limousine height to upturned palm will tear
the very fabric of our society don't you see
that Lord don't you see the dilemma and the
terrible pain of this poor little rich man who
suspects but does not know for sure that out
there in the streets outside his limousine
window is a huge industry diabolically put
together by strategists and sociologists of rare
cunning and creative directors of the devil's

own studio turning out a compelling brand of
designer beggary evoking cleverly targeted
responses from different audiences ranging
from visiting American tycoon to neo-rich
Maruti-800 owners with well-crafted and rehearsed mendicants of different kinds for you
can take your pick from among a spectrum of
the most powerful stimuli whether it is the
oil-painted wound and art-directed sore or
sawed off limb or the limb twisted at birth to
make a deep begging bowl for the future or
the well-rounded and exposed bosom which
is an all time best seller or when they spot a
talent for histrionics you can have your Saint
Vitus Dancer or half-wit man or woman doing his or her thing and this Montblanc
wielding industrialist would perhaps learn
that if he so desired he could buy any one of
these flesh-and-blood works of art for a price
and they would earn for him a profit on the
streets every day and this poor little rich man
looks up to You and says to You it is not fair
it is not right that he has to pay for his well-

pressed suit and his gleaming motor car with
those bruises on his conscience every time he
refuses a beggar a coin which bruise by bruise

has got hardened into cold indifferent stone
not wood and then how will you judge him
Lord now and on that day of trumpet blast
and why Lord should that camel not pass
through the eye of the needle to let this lim-
ousine-blessed could-be benefactor enter the

kingdom while I walk the streets free and
easy picking whatever I can wherever I can
find it I who have hardened the soles of my
feet and the lining of my belly and of my
lungs and dare I tell you of my mind and
conscience and heart because in the sweat-
swapping closeness of breadlines and pavement bedrooms and the rough push and
shove of gruff knife-point prompted orders
from other masters other gods of the night
will you grudge me my moments of survival
and sustenance and triumph and pleasure I
ask of you forgive me father for I have sinned
it is one day since my last moment of surviv-
al-sustenance-triumph-pleasure forgive me
for I have sinned will you and will God and
will His Son write with his finger on the
ground his absolution as to her who was
caught in adultery or will He ask me to wash
in the neighboring *nullah* which is all the
Jordan I can find in the city tell me will He or
won't He or will He exhort me to listen to the
hell-fire sermons that still fill my ears and

decide to prove them true or is it up to me in
some way to climb up that sycamore tree and
then He'll touch me perhaps but when O
Lord when will that hand be on my shoulder
I ask as the rich man's overflow is dished out
to me in my makeshift plate of last week's
newspaper and I take it to a corner and unseen sign myself with the cross of the Grace-
before taught to me by my mother a long
time ago and as the growls in my belly are
made more urgent by the appetizing aroma
of good food I take a big morsel and stuff it
into my mouth and ooh the unspeakable delight of that first big handful of good well
prepared food ah I am going to enjoy this my
Lord I was hungry Lord excruciatingly hungry and now this heaven-prepared food is
doing things to my senses even before I can
take my second morsel yes I know I am going
to eat this banquet not quickly but slowly yes
I will look closely at every grain of the perfectly fried rice bringing rivulets of saliva into
my lower jaw while I caress the food in my

hands to feel the greasy warmth yes and I will take the food in slow-motion up to my mouth yes and I will feel the morsel on my tongue and chew it Oh so slowly savoring the flavor and rolling the texture and tastes of all those spices around my palate and only when I have experienced the full pleasure of that morsel will I permit it to go down yes thank you thank you Lord and now for that second morsel after I swallow this one oh yes I can anticipate the pleasure of that one because I was hungry very hungry O Lord but oh no no no wait a minute for what do I see Oh no I see coming slowly hobbling on aged feet that old man who speaks to nobody and who slapped me on my face last week for bumping into him by mistake that old man from another pavement who has no friends because of his surly nature and terrible countenance and who sits in one place for hours without food or drink till some other pavement dweller puts some morsel in front of him now I see him dragging his feet to where the

food is being dished out and I feel good for
him knowing that he will get some sustenance today from the same bounty that is
feeding me but as I turn round to look at the
food being served I see the last of the baskets
and the last plate being spooned out to some
one else and the old man looks with head
bent to one side while his hunger pangs can
be heard with every step he takes amplified
by my own conscience and then my hand
freezes half-way to my mouth and the fingers
of my hand with the second morsel loosen
and the lining in my belly becomes steel as I
walk to the old man who looks at me a long
time with glazed eyes before he stretches out
his hand when I offer the newspaper plate to
him and while his Adam's apple goes up and
down on his first morsel Lord I lay my body
down to sleep

Pater Noster

Here in the corner of this pavement
I am seething O Lord and I wring
my mind over a past I cannot
change for try as I might I cannot heal the
hurt by fingering my wounds I know I know
but I do so regardless of that realization and
they open up afresh and my fists clench and
my brain aches and my blood boils and my
whole being trembles with impotence as I ask
with angst why he who fathered me fathered
me I demand to know why he had to pass on
to me the genetic design which he himself

would one day curse and then disown I ask O
Lord why did he have to cradle in his affec-
tions and nurture in me a nature which he
would later torment and scourge with word
and deed and an attitude which slid from the
peaks of paternal pride to depths of irritation
and shame tracing a path in my own fall from
parental favor and all because his tunnel vision of my genius was different from my own
my Lord O my Lord should I call you Father
and superimpose on You the ogre image that
fills me with dread and resentment and hurt
and burning anger my Lord and can I still see
in that name that halo of divinity and unend-
ing love and should I still be able to lift my
upturned palms to you in a furtive beggary
enveloped in some dark night of solitude and
inward pain yes I who even during the pangs
of a stomach empty for a yearlong week never did stretch my hand out to ask for the public paisa should I beg now from this limitless
vacuum for my daily sustenance of serenity
and fortitude and a semblance if possible of

justice and of dignity and plain human
warmth which is all that little morsel of your
kingdom I crave on earth in this country in
this city and on this pavement as it is in your
heaven where I may within the spaces of my
own private sin and grief and remorse or
even desire and ambition eat the bread of
stillness and nothingness as once I had tasted
on a sniffed-up high Oh the remembered
bliss of once upon that time which in paren-
thesis I have to put behind me now as I sit
here in my careless corner sucking on a cigarette stub watching the more respectable folk
walk past me with busy gait and furrowed
brow and I wonder how much of the past are
they carrying with them as personal baggage
and am I right in sensing even in the silk-
wrapped roundness of the bellies that go
bobbing by the same tangled web of resentment and guilt and fear and hurt and angst
and impatience and hate and despair or is it
just plain greed for what the present has in
store which brings to mind the catechism of

that desert experience and its sermon to the Satan in all of us about man not living by bread alone but then please let us have in the heat and dust of this stone and asphalt wilderness every word that comes out from Your mouth not second-hand from some theo-illogical pulpit but straight from Your many and perhaps disguised channels of distribution which we may recognize even through the rude and vulgar exteriors and expressions that we are accustomed to on this pavement as coming from Your mouth if I can see it for even now while I sit and view the ruins of the fortress that once was my self-esteem I rue the day I discovered my rare gifts of hand and voice and intellect and so did my parents and in time the neighborhood and my teachers and fellow students looking in awe at my many talents whether they were the fluid lines that flowed from lead point or nib or plain stick on mud that traced patterns and shapes and likenesses right out of my head for I was gifted with a hand that could

reproduce the visions in my head and with an
eye that could pick out the little features that
made one face different from another and I
could put them down on paper with a flourish and so they marveled at this talent and at
the wide sweep of my general knowledge
which I picked up like a thirsty sponge from
books that they had not even seen or my gift
of declamation and dramatic expression but
even more the ease with which I cleared my
classes with the best grades and all with the
greatest of ease yes I had them all blowing
around me a balloon of expectations that got
bigger with every triumph and its resulting
applause and I in my own world of butterfly
fantasies flitting from one dream to another
on the wings of my own changing desires and
feelings untied to reason or ambition was
lured by the attraction of the visual arts and
all those magic wands of nib and point and
sable hair all the time devouring those stories
of the lives of the artists and wanting to be
like them even living in my imagination the

life of Toulouse-Lautrec and Van Gogh and
Picasso and for a time as late as my adoles-
cence even going barefooted like Hussain oh
yes I wanted with all my heart to be an artist
not stopping for a moment to think of the
social hierarchy of talent because all I saw on
my horizon were the colors and shapes of a
world that I would create from the energies
that seemed to be bursting forth from my
brain and heart and viscera demanding to be
born unmindful of all those clicking tongues
and shaking heads around me bemoaning the
fizzling out of so much intellectual dynamite
and the sad waste of a would-be leader of society or at least of one who would certainly be
rolling as they said in it because I could be
rich and famous they said if only I pursued
the path that society respected and rewarded
with money and status and respectability and
if I was not stupid enough to follow a line
that was at best good only as a pastime or a
hobby and they shook their heads in anger
and disbelief as I decided to enroll in an art

school rather than in a science or commerce college but then who but You should know the strong tugs of my own inner calling and the youthful disdain and the finality with which I flung away all the opinions and advice of older people who said that I was spoilt by my parents who treated me like a prima donna and serves them right because see where all that spoiling has taken me and that should well be a lesson for all parents with gifted children and so on and so forth and yet I did not budge from my decision and now so many years after the event should I ask if You did at that moment give me Your divine guidance in some whispered form or compelling circumstance and was my seemingly stubborn decision preordained by you and if it was something you let me do then why O why Lord am I in this pit of degradation and spiritual despair today I ask of you Lord where is it written that all those who follow the heart and the gut to express what is within them must end up as social disasters tell

me Lord what links the aesthetic sensibility
with brothels and pawnbrokers and even
chopped off ears or even if one ignores the
biases of a mundane and materialistic society
tell me Lord is such talent always cursed by
You to walk the streets or will You tell me
that it is quite the other way around that you
bestow on them the martyrdom reserved for
saints by pushing them to invest their pain in
the aesthetic heritage of the world but there I
go again beatifying my misdemeanors with
maudlin argument and in any case what does
that matter now that things have turned out
the way they have I ask should I put the
blame on the pointing finger of Destiny or do
I say Thy will be done as if Gethsemane were
here and now or is it Gabbatha in other
words the Pavement of Pilate's judgment seat
condemning me to be scourged for the blas-
phemy of my own angle of view now long
past its relevance to anyone I sit here on this
pavement washed in drain-water and the release of bursting bladders that could not wait

and on this dark night of remembrance and
hurt Lord is it up to me to say a Father forgive me or is it forgive them as I do for they
knew yes they knew what they were doing
and I did not so help me God and erase from
your book the blotched pages of my mistakes
and if I dare look at today and tomorrow can
I make so bold as to ask you to direct my
steps away from the paths of the past and can
I blank out yesterday's pain and right yesterday's wrong by turning up my palms to a
starless sky offering up my wounds like stig-
mata from a crucifixion which I deserved like
one of the two on either side of Salvation and
will the promise of Paradise be addressed to
me or the other I wonder

The Angelus

Last week I found a new address for myself after having moved all these years from one corner of a borrowed shelter and earned relationships to another and that not so much because I wanted more comfort and personal space for myself as because I seemed to have become a displaceable thing in the eyes of those around me as also I must admit out of my own choice and though it seemed that I was an easy eviction and a willing victim of pavement bullies I found it easier and indeed inwardly liberating with

each eviction to just pick up my belongings
and look for the few square meters I needed
in another patch of friendly pavement in time
realizing that for many it was not the dis-
placement of the corporeal frame and its
physical demands that caused pain but the
ejection of the ego which for me seemed almost to not exist with regard to material ac-
quisitions at least yet my Lord never once
did I bring to mind your gospel poetry of the
foxes and their holes and the birds and their
nests and the Son of Man with no place to lay
his head yes I confess I was no imitation of
your redemptive rambling my Lord rather in
the eyes of my pavement acquaintances I was
one who had lost all focus and spirit and the
will to live indeed was one who drifted from
one blank page to another leaving not a mark
behind and yet I can tell you and perhaps you
alone that this seemingly mindless detach-
ment and lack of personal preference for possessions and emotional niches for myself is
strangely opening up within me growing

spaces of untouched whiteness like a canvas waiting to be filled and I feel a calmness spread inside me as I sit down in my new little corner watching the mostly lazy routine of my new neighbors like the early morning clatter of buckets as Neha who is perhaps in her late teens has an open-air bath on the pavement ingeniously tying a length of cloth a little over her very buxom bosom while with a cake of laundry soap she whips up an amazing lather in her hair and then later with her eyes closed to avoid the dripping soap water she rubs down her whole body including the spaces inside that length of cloth with perfectly practiced modesty so no vulgar eye can feast on the portions she wants to keep out of lecherous visual consumption shuddering at the first mug of cold water over her head but later reveling in the refreshing coolness of her bath and when she is through with half the bucket she squeezes out the water from her hair and ties it into a bun behind her head and starts dressing up without even

wiping her body dry for that is a function
that has to be performed by the clothes she
puts on and now it is Gomti's turn with the
remaining half of the bucket that will disap-
pear faster and with less of a ritual than in
Neha's case because Gomti says she believes
in looking presentable without having to
make too much of a fuss about it because she
has no use now for the admiring glances of
those brutes she took in during her brothel
days which started when she was no more
than a girl and went on for far too long with
always that promise of easy wealth and even
stardom which some of those lying dogs held
out to her as they tried to extract as much as
they could from her body and now she
thanked her favorite god who in his time did
hide the clothes of the bathing gopis but who
had in her own life-time in answer to her devotion saved her from the sickly grip of that
terrible calling to let her try her hand at other
more self-respecting professions and now
though she was reduced to life on the pave-

ment she was at least surrounded as far as she could see by men who looked at her with some respect because they were good men at heart yes they were good men like that gentle giant of our pavement whom we called Dondu and who could always be relied on to fetch

and carry things and to stand up for them
against the bullies from other localities but
who she believed could make better use of his
gifts than to sit down there with Fatfatia and
polish the shoes of the city because somebody
should honestly tell him that he did not have
Fatfatia's charm with people or even his way
with shoes for when it comes down to servic-
ing the vanity of men you have to know how
to exploit it beginning with that slight but
visible curl of the nose as you glance at the
dirty leather passing by as if it were some
stale fish in a çathedral's sanctuary and the
timely tap of the brush on the shoe stand or
that flurry of applications of polish and
cream and spit in one continuous whirl of
stylish gesture and that flourish of the brush
and cloth like a conductor's baton at the fina-
le yes Fatfatia was a true artist and showman
at his shoe-stand but Dondu was just ear-
nestness laid on with brute force and he never even stopped to wonder why Fatfatia
would earn twice as much as he on any given

day which is why Kalia would often invite
Dondu to join him at the docks where they
took on muscular looking men for lifting and
hauling goods saying that with his looks he
would be the first to be picked by the clearing
agents any day and then there was Ganga
who had just recently moved in as it were on
a request from Fatfatia to Gomti to keep her
till he had enough money to marry her but
Gomti knew as did everyone else that Fatfatia
expected us to close our collective eye to their
nocturnal moments of conjugal embrace and
I wonder my God if they could count on you
too to look the other way and not insist on
those rites of the sacred knot and fire before
the eyes of men to proclaim to the world
what you have planted in their breast I wonder as I witness the warm and easy relationships around me I sense a feeling of quiet awe
towards me because not one of them can un-
derstand why a person like me has landed on
the streets with the likes of them for they
have seen me with my books and my art ma-

terial and they have listened with respect as if
to a guru as I have spoken to them Lord I feel
grateful for their sensitivity to the way I am
for they allow me my space and I have seen
them hush the children up into silence when
they have seen me reading my books yes I
am grateful for all this and even now as I
watch the scene before me I spy Ganga on the
other side of the street on the pavement opposite ours bow down as she strikes a bell at
the makeshift altar to Hanuman which is as
good as a mini-temple where so many pass-
ersby through the day stop and ring that bell
bringing to my mind those metal muezzins of
our parish steeple and belfry at noon and
dusk calling the faithful to pray and remind-
ing us in particular to celebrate in that moment of frozen activity the mystery of your
incarnation in rattled off rote and now I see a
wonderful reversal of that call in which the
faithful on the other side of the road clang
out their calls to their god asking that he heed
their presence and come down to them on

that pavement and amid the reverberations of
the Om and the ringing of the bells I visualize
for my own spirit the Word becoming flesh
right there on the street in front of me

Confiteor

Kalia confessed to murder last night amid a hushed silence which lasted only a short while before he went into a detailed account of the events that led to it nine years ago in his village in Bihar where his wife's secret lover had taken him for a walk in the fields and they both shared a bidi and spoke to each other like good friends when on a sudden Kalia saw the man reach into his dhoti and pull out his sickle and come at him aiming for the back of his throat but not before Kalia stepped swiftly aside and caught the murderous hand and twisted it with such force that the sickle fell to the ground and in the panic of the moment Kalia

picked it up while his other hand held fast to the man's wrist and before he knew it he found the newly sharpened blade of the sickle half-way through the neck of his attacker and to this day Kalia swears that his hand performed the bloody deed of its own volition from the severing of the head to the burying of the body in a marsh covered over with reeds and after a few days of guilt and fear when he almost gave himself up to the police who were investigating the case but half-heartedly because the missing man was a no-body in that village except to his wife he told his family that he was going to Calcutta to look for a job but took a train to Mumbai instead and has lived here ever since in different parts of the city and now on this pavement with us and I vouch for him O God in heaven there has not been a gentler soul so I know you will look with kindness on his past because his crime which the authorities have not detected is worthy of the ultimate punishment but the sin may well be washed clean

in the flood of a more knowing and divine
justice and you should have seen his face
when he had finished his story and everyone
in the group stared at him in shades of shock
which they tried to hide to save him from
feeling terrible Kalia looked across at Mamta
like an errant child before his mother and
asked her if she now utterly loathed him and
would never speak to him because of what he
had done and while everyone waited to hear
what she would say she drew the pallu of her
sari over her head and looked down at the
pavement as if the answer were written there
and she began tracing imaginary circles on it
with her finger as she muttered under her
breath that the rest of us were no saints and
quietly proceeded to tell us of the violence
between her and her parents over a boy she
was infatuated with in her village only a few
years ago when she was mad enough to believe that Brahma himself had formed this
creature from some rare material to be part of
her life for never a waking moment would

pass without his face coming before her eyes
and his voice in her ear and even at night she
would wake up actually feeling the touch of
his hand all over her body coaxing her to be
part of him causing her whole being to burn
with the wanting of him and when it got too
much to bear she spoke to her parents about
it who went into fits of rage particularly her
father who hurled curses and abuse at her for
daring to make a choice on her own yes even
today she could hear very clearly the hurtful
and ugly words she had flung at them during
the fight and how her drunken father had
lunged at her and had ripped open her blouse
exposing her bosom to his bloodshot eyes
and how when he approached her again to
lay his hands on her she had pushed the man
with all her force against the wall feeling
strong and triumphant and almost glad when
he fell unconscious and how she ran away
with her lover to the city where after a time
he the dog that he was he left her for an older
woman leaving her to fend for herself be-

cause she was too proud to go back to her
parents and when her story was finished
there were other true stories told by others on
that close-knit pavement of transgression and
contrite acknowledgement of personal weak-
ness and iniquity and when they had all finished their confessions and were given the
group's unspoken absolution they looked at
me and asked aloud how an educated and
talented person like me came to be one of
them and I still wrapped up in the rags of my
own intellect now worn out and threadbare
felt it hard to join in the act of community
reconciliation which the others had slipped
into so naturally but I was moved as it were
by their expectancy which bore no malice to
confess what you O lord know already but
which now in the spirit of the moment am
impelled to give expression to for the first
time before this communion of your saints
and my friends not asking to be understood
or condoned nor holding up the jagged
blackness of my life to the seeming whiteness

of the ladies and gentlemen who trot past on
upright sounding heels across this pavement

to I do not know what convent of decency I
reach back to what I can remember of those
times when I wielded pointed lead and crow-

quill and sable hair on Kent paper to push
commerce and earn a living yet feeling all the
while that what I wanted to do was something different from what I produced on that
sleepy easel feeling that there was something
infinitely big within me that I had not
touched yet with my mind or crow-quill or
brush and that I was wasting my time doing
what I was doing although around me there
were paeans of praise being sung by my boss
and my peers about my talent and the work
that I was doing which to me seemed like
things that really did not matter never for a
moment agreeing with the elders that so
much intellectual vanity and ambition was as
good as looking the divine gift-horse in the
mouth tantamount to the sin of ungrateful-
ness to God they said but I felt dissatisfied
with myself and unfulfilled till that day in
that tea shop I saw this unkempt foreign
white skinned young man flecked with days
of unwashed city grime who was sipping his
tea with a faraway look in his eye and whom

the others pointed out as a hippie which he was complete with beard and a back-pack from which he fished out sheets of paper on which were drawn with pen and ink the most fascinating pictures I had ever seen combining grace of line and boldness of design with the most bizarre and surprising mix of figures

in which the erotic and the mystical seemed
to become one and that created within me a
strange feeling of release and tension and as I
looked at one drawing after another he told
me that he had many more pictures like these
and I could see them if I went over with him
to where he lived and I did and there amid
the dirt and mess of that room he introduced
me to his art and to his girl friend more unkempt and wilder than he and while I was
being mesmerized by the flowing lines of his
drawings I got the whiff of smoke which
smelt strange and I asked him what it was
that he was smoking and he said it was the
stuff that drew the lines for him on his sheets
of paper and he inhaled with a fury till the
cigarette burnt his fingers and then he took
pen and ink and drew almost in a trance
some more of those hypnotic pictures and
then he offered me a cigarette which I accepted with some trepidation but an equal excitement and the three of us filled the room
with that strange smoke and I saw or imag-

ined I saw the most fantastic lines in my head
and that was only the beginning of my experiments with those mind-bending drugs which
I inhaled and swallowed and sniffed and in-
jected into my system and in that limbo of
my unconsciousness of those times I scarcely
remember what I did or thought nor even
about those loud and terrible fights I had
with my family and my father who on one of
those violent occasions threw all my clothes
at me in a bundle and showed me the door
and I walked out in a temper swearing to
them amid the tear-stained entreaties of my
mother and sister that I would never return
and when I stopped going home for the
nights and started living with the foreign
couple it was one long blank space dotted
with half-remembered sequences of strolls
through dark lanes in the city and meetings
with other hippies creating as it were out of
those hardly conscious moments a dark tunnel of drug-induced forgetting and yet I remember that day after a drug-soaked after-

noon the girl slipped out of all her clothes and asked the two of us to sketch her body which we did in our own different styles and when I looked at his sketch it was nothing like her with no likeness of face or the shape of her body but just a continuation of the fantastic lines he had always drawn and mine was a realistic rendering of her body down to her features in detail and she took both the drawings and left the room for half and hour or so returning with only the picture he had drawn and she asked me to do another and I did and every day after that while her partner went out into the city she would ask me to do my sketches of her till one day I saw her at a street corner hawking her nude pictures and I saw that the ones in demand were the ones I had done of her because of the sensuality of that realism to curious eyes and so every day I sketched the lines of her body and then one day after the drawing was over we lit ourselves a cigarette and another and another and when we were in a thick mist of unknowing she led me to her body and fed me with ecstasies which in that zone of unmeasured time seemed to go on and on like one endless climax and day after day for I do not know how many days after that how many weeks and months and years it was for me one continuous unreality of impossible pleasure and as I see now four decades later my beard grown gray through the thick clouds of unremembering I dread to even call your name O Lord for I cannot recall when the two disappeared from my life and when the other hippies became my companions admitting me to their small smelly rooms and heavier doses of those mind-warping drugs and I do not know how many years it was when the cloud lifted and I saw that I was on the streets looking at pictures which I had done and which were no different from what I had always done only they were worse having lost all form and meaning and when I put pencil to paper then I realized that my hands trembled and my mind was an aching blank and

all I could do was limp through the streets
with yesterday on my back and now in this
pavement confessional where you and your
saints and my friends can look with pity on
an aging sinner will you O Lord send me to
my doom I ask seeing albeit dimly the answer
in the response of that pavement brotherhood for when I had finished my confession I
felt a calm spreading across the group like an
invisible holding of hands for many moments
till Mamta opened her cloth bag and took out
from it a pile of chappattis and distributed to
us all and we munched in that silence of an
assured brotherhood

The Litany

Lord my palms are hurting and in places bleeding but I have to go on you see I have to keep tugging at this thick coir rope of which each fibre feels like the edge of a blunt knife scraping against my flesh as I hold tight and pull with all my might and with all my weight behind it because today Lord I have got myself some work which means I have got myself some food thank you God yes thank you but then do my fingers have to bleed before I pick up a morsel I ask you Lord do they have to hurt

just so my stomach gets its consolation tell
me do you do this to every one in need of a
comforted belly were you serious in your
Eden speech about the sweat of the brow and
the trickle of the bleeding palm in some form
or the other I ask you I'm sorry lord for there
I go again but you know me and you know I
was not brought up to hard labour no they
didn't teach me to pull a rope in all the five
years of art school no they didn't ask me to so
much as exert the muscles beyond those
around my finger-tips so I could trace with a
number-one sable hair Winsor and Newton
brush point the curlicues that made up those
eyelashes of the nude in front of the class and
here I am today pulling with both hands lean-
ing Pisa-like to one side almost on my heels
to deposit my weight where my muscles fall
short of the force needed for the job forming
together with the thirty other pullers of the
rope parallel obliques against a dusty background filling the air with the accidental
harmony of unequal voices but with perfect

rhythm intoning that litany of the straining muscle that *ayyaaaare-oomba-oomba-ayyaaaare-oomba-oomba* with each tug feeling in that resonating sound inside my belly the surge of power from that baritone register of *ayya-re-oomba-oomba* and soon I am pretending that it's not my muscles I am using but my voice and I feel better and become oblivious of the sweat on my brow and the crimson trickle on my palms and the tautness in my biceps and calf muscles ayyaaa-re-oomba-oomba the rope tightens into a straight line going diagonally up to one end of the huge metal pole they are erecting for I don't even know what purpose with the other end firmly wedged into the ground held by strong metal hinges which help the pole to rise with each tug and labour litany ayaaa-re-oomba-oomba my mind fixed on the nothingness of a barely moving pole floats on to a blankness which makes me feel one with the earth and sky and the strong energising odour of perspiration and the sounds of the

air and the resonating Litany of the Straining
Muscle ayyaaa-re-oomba-oomba as my mind
is emptied of all thought and in that empti-
ness grows and extends beyond the boundaries that were drawn by my own continuous
line of thinking ayyaaa-re-oomba-oomba into a boundless firmament of nothingness and
peace dispelling all consciousness of torn
flesh and jagged feelings lifting me higher
with the sound of my litany ayyaaa-re-oomba
vaguely as through a mist I see the pole almost erect now pointing up to the clouds like
a proud finger borrowing its triumph from
the sweat of our brow and the trickle of our
palms pointing up not looking down to the
flesh and blood and sinews that lifted it upward yes I think now of all those proud tall
fingers of chrome and concrete which make
the cityscape pointing always higher and
higher and not looking for a moment down
and around at the those whose sweat gives
strength to concrete and as I line up now for
those few soiled currency notes carefully sep-

arated with spittle soaked digits and doled
out into our aching palms I wonder if these
offspring of Babel's continuing ambition
would ever rise even one foot up without the
Litany of the Straining Muscle

Via Crucis

On Wednesday they brought Fat-fatia's ashes home if home you could call that address on the pavement yes my Lord they brought them in an earthen pot tied to a string handle all the way from the crematorium near the prison where he had spent the past three months waiting for his case to come up for the trial that in the end was not to be as our dear friend Fatfatia was brought to this prison from another where earlier he had spent two bruised months which left marks upon and inside his body the visible and invisible evidence of attempts to draw out from his innocence a confession of the rape which you know O Lord and I know and even the police know Lord that he did not commit but someone had to be held up to satisfy the public clamour for what they know as justice as always someone has to be nailed for all time and for all eyes to see that Justice's flabby body has at least been stirred up from its somnolence even if it was set in motion by an unknowing careless finger pointed towards a soft target on the pavement to the accompaniment of brandishing batons and blows of brutish fists rained hard on crouched innocence O Lord I screamed at them and protested his innocence but they shut me up with fists in my face even while Dondu our pavement muscle man ran up to the crouched figure and covered that bleeding body with his own and took the batons and the lashes and the pounding fists on his back and on his arms for a full fifteen minutes Dondu big

Dondu wonder Dondu our hero Dondo bless
him Lord held fast to his friend and taunted
and challenged the scourging hands to do
their worst and they did till fifteen hands of
the devil struggled to loosen the grip of true
friendship and pull victim and protector
apart and then screaming Ganga streaming
tears on muddy cheeks ran up to the barely
moving body with a battered mug of water in
one hand and she lifted his head up to wash
his face and wipe it with her dupatta before
those fifteen hands of the devil came down
again on her and dragged her away by her
hair while all the others stood around looking
at the scene like a street play yes their faces all
alive with interest as if gripped by some third
rate movie yes and their eyes moving from
one dramatis persona to another as if antici-
pating the next move in a cleverly written
plot and I said to myself and I ask you my
Lord why does another's pain provide us with
so much detached interest and how does flesh
and blood bear to look at flesh and blood be-

ing torn and spilt and not lift finger or voice
in succour and how is it that we can look and
click our tongues in pity and stand paralysed
and dumb so we can go away when it is all
over and tell our friends and acquaintances of
the injustice and the inhumanity of some
people and the pain of the victim and we can
speak piously and even with righteous sounding anger of the terrible state of our society
and we say our prayers to a God who we
think did not see our inaction when right
there and then while Injustice and Inhumanity were playing their stellar roles in front of
us we were and will always be spectators at
the many stations of our brother's suffering
and so urged on by my own guilt at standing
apart I rushed to his aid mindlessly but with
emotion and I was dragged away and struck
and handcuffed together with him and driven
off to jail and on the way and inside those
caged confines I felt a strange sense of calm
Lord at being able to share Fatfatia's humilia-
tion and his pain unmindful of what was

happening outside the prison till Dondu came one day and told me what they had done to Ganga who for the past many days has been refusing food and drink saying that she would rather die because of what was done to her by those cowardly men who stripped her in the dead of night and did their heinous deed and left her half dead and naked on the rocks till she was discovered in her shame by her own people who had come looking out for her and I told Dondu not to speak of it to Fatfatia for who knows what it would do to him who knows it would make him lose his senses and cause him to grow violent and then there was no knowing what would happen Lord Lord why do you let things like these happen to innocent people why Lord do you forsake them in their hour of need I ask and does the suffering innocent always have to lay the bruised body and spirit at the doorstep of your unshakeable will hoping for some form of reward and is it fair to expect from finite endurance that fortitude to

accept the larger plan of an infinite justice I
ask O Lord for now I hear that Fatfatia has
been taken to the prison hospital for treatment of the severe wounds that have been
inflicted all these days in order to extract a
confession and I am released from prison because they do not have a serious enough case
against me so I go to see Fatfatia in hospital
and can hardly believe my eyes at the sight of
him for his eyes are black and swollen and he
has welts all over his body but I am told that
the greater damage has been done inside to
his bones and his internal organs and the
doctors quietly shake their heads as they
move away and the journalists push their way
past the rough policemen and bend down
close to Fatfatia's face and ask him details of
the police brutality so that they can write all
about it and expose the guilty ones but he
smiles and shakes his head feebly and tells
them to forget it because it is all of no use and
then he sees me and calls me to him and ex-
tracts a promise which I agree to readily to

look after his mother and I think of my own who with my Father and older brother has left the shores to settle down in New Zealand I was told and now because of Fatfatia I have a mother yes I tell him yes don't worry my friend your mother has another son called John and it was a little after that that he breathed his last and he was cremated and his ashes brought home and while the men sobbed and the women tore their hair there came into my fingers a force I had not felt for a long time and I dug into my old bag and fished out the pieces of crayon from it and quickly with strokes that came from my heart I put down his portrait on the wall right there behind our pavement and they watched till their eyes dried up and they stood still around it and slowly they went down on their knees and bowed down to the ground as if to a great guru and an alleluia rose up from my heart

An Examination
of Conscience

arly this morning I saw Pandu park
his car and start his jog in starched
white shorts and T-shirt while I was
buying my cup of tea from Gomti who has of
late set up a kerosene stove on the pavement
which is now her little breakfast stall serving
us with hot tea for fifty paise per cup and for
those of us who can afford it fried eggs or
omelette or even potato and onion bhajias
demonstrating for us her new claim of being
a better cook than the whore she was and as

the steaming cup woke up my senses I saw
Pandu panting and streaming with sweat
coming back for another round of his jog and

after he had finished his morning exercise he
walked towards his car wiping his face with a

hand towel when his eyes moving over to
where I was met mine and for an instant I
could sense the hesitation in his mind before
he came over to where I was and spoke to me
and told me that he had over the years
watched from a distance my spiraling slide to
damnation and that he being involved with
the twists and turns in his own life could
hardly stop to even speak to me for life had
moved fast for him from the time he was the
tea boy in our office right up to when he took
over the pantry from his boss and had made
enough money to get out and try his hand at
other bigger and more daring ventures some
of them dangerously slippery because of the
stubborn stupidity of the law as he put it but
then he was sharp enough to dodge both the
police and the underworld to make it big first
as an intermediary in goods that leaked out of
cargo ships at the docks and later as a building contractor and today his family of four
are living a comfortable life heaven be praised
in one of the apartments in the city that he

owns and then when he had finished narrat-
ing his story he looked down at me with a
mixture of pity and scorn and asked me why

I with all my talent could not lift myself out
of the rut and the mess I was in and why did I
have to continue living in this environment
of sin and sinners and he went on to talk to

me about paap and punya and the conse-
quences of my karma and how I had wasted
by life in the gutters and when this had gone
on for some time I could feel my mind
switching off before he even left me and I got
to thinking about my life on this pavement
where the hand and eye have learnt to fend
for the rest of the body in whatever manner is
expedient like in war yes this is war of the
most desperate kind where the line between
work and crime is a thin mist because survival is a law greater than politeness because the
screams of the flesh are more urgent than the
whispers of conscience where the requisitions
sent out by the pangs of hunger and the pal-
pitations of fear and the urgent throbbing of
arousal need to be addressed with minimum
expense on this pavement where fornication
is fine and frequent and sleight of hand in
another's pocket is seen as artistry and the
wristy grip on another's throat is derring-do
tell me Lord can we do any wrong any more
than those uniformed regiments who get

decorated for every hundred souls they snuff
out and every wife and daughter they deflow-
er in the name of territorial greed and survival of another kind Lord will you not find
reasonable excuse for Thambi and Savitri
sleeping together in sweaty embrace without
that piece of paper called a marriage license
in their pockets or their ten year-old bastard
son's legerdemain with wallets of all kinds
and the buxom bosom that Neha nicely lets
slip out of her choliless sari feigning a dis-
traught mind to the greedy eyes of white men
in taxis to extract that heavy note from their
pockets or Purnima who is similarly endowed
but accomplishes her task by pretending to
feed a two year-old child she has borrowed
for the purpose why do I take it for granted
and accept it all like the rest of this pavement
as part of life's necessities Lord and will you
send them to damnation to a weeping and
wailing and gnashing of teeth other than
what they are already heir to but should
there not be a different catechism and a

Pavement Apologetics perhaps that will tilt
the scales of judgement day in a more equita-
ble distribution of hell-fire or should the
punishment for the sins of this pavement be
visited not on the pavement but on the cir-
cumstances that created it or should I be so
imprudent and so brash as to point an accusing finger at that accumulation of circum-
stances we call society and even hint that it is
in fact the Original Sin of the city made visible on the pavement through its injustice
and   inequalities and the indifference and
carelessness and callousness and corruption
and selfishness and greed and the incompe-
tence of those in office and the general blind-
ness of the city to the amount of flesh and
blood in the city sewer Oh no Lord here I go
again taking on myself the examination of the
city's conscience by counting my companions
and myself not as the criminals but the crime
for heaven's sake not the sinners but the sins
committed by this vast attractive metropolis
and the people who run it and declaiming in

my best Sunday Gospel reading voice that in
the beginning was the Sin and the Sin was in
the City and the Sin was the City and each
one of us on this pavement is the city's sin
made flesh dwelling amongst you my dear
brethren can you not see we are the devil's
laughing parody of John's First Chapter but
how does an entire city beat its breast in a
collective mea culpa I ask my God unless you
work the great miracle in 18 million separate
hearts suddenly gripped by their own conscience even as I now in the course of my
own retreat seek to delve into my own past
now there is so much of it behind me and ask
you Lord what sin have I been guilty of I who
have never harmed a soul as far as I can remember and you know I have never slipped
my hand into another's pocket or taken what
was not my due even through starvation and
hard times will you damn me for the youthful
experiments with those mind-bending substances and those sensual journeys I took
with one and then other willing partners who

opened up for me paths of pleasure unknown to me because not one of those delights were stolen but were surrendered freely in a mutual giving of one's body to the other and yet today as I sit here alone with these questions and the easy logic of the pavement in my head I feel the disturbing twinges caused by the catechism in my marrow which conjures up visions of Sinai and tablets of stone and the mystical body which has to be kept in one piece and then my mind goes back even further to sins that were visible to nobody because they happened within the curtained stage of my own ego and in my heart and in the convolutions of word and interaction with those who were part of my growing years and it is these seemingly small and invisible non-events which are beginning to hurt in my memory because distanced by time I can now see the trail of pain they left behind and while my mind now maps the territory of my arrogance over the years I

view each episode with the magnification of
an aging man's introspection

Act of Contrition

I feel it rise up from deep within me like another self pushing to be born to take over all that I was until now because it has taken me a long time to say this Lord but I do it now with my whole being yes my God I say it because it comes now from a profound realization of the hurts I left behind I say that I am sorry I am deeply sorry and this feeling of remorse is a new experience for me my God this Great Sorrow filling me with a dazzling white silence and a weightlessness that surprises me as I sit with my head in my hands here in my little corner on this pavement sensing this curtain lift to a vision of Light and Knowledge not darkness and despair as I might have expected because I have felt sorry

before this oh yes a hundred and a thousand times before Lord a feeling I put on with as much readiness as that with which I wore my joy or my triumph yes sorrow was easy to slip into like a blanket over my head choking me with a black darkness and a leaden weight over my spirit dragging me down to depths of self-pity and despair and a feeling of persecution and injustice and anger and hate because this was a feeling of sorrow for myself seeking apology from the whole world starting from my parents and moving on to my friends and peers and the establishment and from my God himself because I felt I was the wronged one throughout not always the blameless but always the wronged one and every single fall into these pits of feeling sorry left bruises and hurts and scars on my spirit I know but today I feel like another being I feel like I am all of them yes like I am my own father and mother and brother and sister and friends and teachers and church and society and country yes

like I am the world and the universe itself
feeling the pain of what I have done all these
years puncturing the fabric of Wholeness and
bruising the Infinity of Goodness through the
wounds inflicted on those around me whom I
see now so clearly yes every sling and whip-
lash of tongue and gesture the fast and furious vocabulary of rebellion and defiance and
cynicism and superiority and anger and indifference and ridicule and condescension
with the resulting anguish of those within
hurting distance with the ones closest to me
receiving the harshest blows yes it all comes
back to me like a movie which till now I
viewed only in reverse because the striking
hand was mine and not theirs as I imagined
all these years my God and now I ask you
how long does it take for one to receive this
dazzling white gift of real Sorrow and why is
it that I for years in my post-natal womb of
selfishness was unwilling and unable to be
born to your greater reality and to see that
my remorse ought not to be over what has

become of me today because I have taken my
own steps to this station Lord but in the
marks I have left in your kingdom of peace
and I feel at this point of time after all these
years the need to say I am sorry a thousand
times to you and the many whom I have hurt
and I know them every single one by name
and I sit and go through the seemingly endless sequences of my own villainy from the
days of petty disobedience and sly mischief to
my struts in front of parents and relations
and teachers and peers to the more strident
expressions of my own will which brought to
my father's face as I see clearly now in the
crystal clarity of penitence his contortions of
pain on that day which happened in a whirl
then which is played back in slow motion to
me now I see that day clearly when I came
home disheveled and dirty and reeking of the
drugs that I had ingested in the company of
my friends of the street when I hurled abuse
and insult and the devil's own thesaurus at
my family yes they looked at me with that

look of unbelief and pain with tears streaming down the cheeks of my mother and sister
and my father who in a moment of harsh decision collected all my clothes and belongings
and flung them at me and asked me to leave
home and all I remember at that time was my
own anger and sense of persecution but today
I can feel in my bones the wrenching pain of
the man as if he O Lord was obeying your
command to cut of that limb that caused him
to do wrong and knowing that I was that limb
that had to be sawed off for the greater good
of the body I can see it all till I arrive at my
long drug-induced blank which I came out of
slowly as through a smoggy day which went
on for years when through the clouds of half
consciousness I experienced confusion of
mind and a hollowness in my flesh and bones
and I felt hunger and pain and the stones
pelted by little urchins and the jibes and
laughter that are hurled at madmen on the
streets and in my own very personal savour-
ing of my act of sorrow I wonder Lord how

many in your world of the sane and the righteous do in the course of their lives actually
walk through the shadow of blankness without knowing it because theirs is a blankness
that fits into the warp and weft of career and
family comfort and social life and may in fact
be a necessary part of it all but then is my experience very different from theirs when they
go through an entire stretch of their roads
quite unconscious of the world outside their
own bubble of ambition and success and
pleasure at all costs and are not these the in-
sidious hallucinogenic drugs of the seemingly righteous erasing all consciousness of other
people other feelings other hopes other
dreams other roads to be taken other goals to
look forward to other things to be done thus
leaving unexplored the vast territory of your
grace and their own gifts yes the many other
channels of peace and joy and fulfillment
which help to complete your act of creation
O God I know it is not for me to ask except to
know that for me it has taken a lifetime of

this self-centred blankness during which time
I know now I inflicted pain on many to come
out of the tunnel of blackness which is the
limbo of my self-containment into the light
of this realization and this eye-opening this
world-opening contrition so help me my God

Credo

Last week Lord I painted a picture of Sai Baba on a stone slab for Ganga who now keeps it in her corner of our pavement and every day someone or the other places flowers or puts a garland around it and they bow their heads and pray to this saint with no religious boundaries and they come to me and thank me and compliment me on the work saying that there is an expression in my Sai Baba's eyes which they have not seen in any other Sai Baba but Ganga believes that it is not I but some divinity

which in all probability must be the God I
believe in that has endowed my fingers with a
super-natural power seeing that this is the
first full painting in oils that I have done
since the days of my commercial art nearly
thirty five years ago now and she has talked
about it to the entire street and all the other
streets in the neighbourhood as a result of
which I have been approached by other
pavement communities and even by a *mitra
mandal* to paint pictures of Hanuman and
Ganapati and Saraswati and Krishna and in
fact I am already half-way through the blue
god now surprised at my own fluency with
the medium unlike Ganga who is convinced
of the divine power in my fingers and asks
me to paint a picture of my own God in other
words the Christian God and I tell her that I
do not know how to paint my God nor do I
need to and she not quite understanding
what I mean fishes out of her blouse a picture of the Sacred Heart of Jesus and one of
the Sacred Heart of Mary to help me and I

shake my head with a smile as I finger the rosary in my pocket if rosary you can call those bits of broken links and the few beads that are left on it and I feel with thumb and forefinger the metal figure of Him crucified on that little cross of wood among the dirt and lint inside my trouser pocket giving shape in that instant to the state of my personal faith broken but there still unseen by the world but felt with thumb and forefinger in the lint-littered corner of my consciousness O Lord my God what strange places do you choose to hide in just to jog the weakening spirit for I have kept those diminishing beads attached to that cross with me for nearly five decades after it was presented to me by my grandmother on the day of my first communion those beads changing pockets only to be with me wherever I went not that I prayed those beads after those daily mutterings we called the family rosary every night but out of habit I must confess Lord a habit like buttoning up my trousers or gulping

down my coffee before leaving home yes
those beads that placed the Holy Trinity with
the Virgin Mary and the communion of
saints on tip of tongue and between thumb
and forefinger all through those altar boy
days of rote-rattled Latin responses of my
habemus ad Dominum to the priest's *sursum
corda* and the May holiday evening rosaries
at the village cross through my days at art
school and commercial art and right through
the hippie limbo years my catechism lay broken in my right hand trouser pocket and in
the space between my closed eyelids and the
black sky of a starless night when I would see
the faint outlines of what was given me at the
font of my baptism so I tend to call on your
name Lord even now so far away from hell-
fire-breathing pulpit and altar rail and pew
and holy water font or chasubled rites I speak
to you in the stream of my unconsciousness
where yet I am not able to see your face if I
have to put you down on a slab of stone to be
counted among the many deities of our

pavement chapel for O Lord is yours the face
that was seen in Eden or the one in Moses'
burning bush or is yours the cherubic face in
the manger in Bethlehem or the one streaming blood on a cross or is yours the face of the
dove over the river Jordan or the face in the
clouds on that last Day of Judgement I do not
know and I cannot explain this to an insistent
Ganga and now the others on this pavement
who need to punctuate the inevitability of
the daily hunger pangs and the casual brawl
and instant fornication and petty crime with
moments of camaraderie and sharing and
once a day at least a personal union with the
gods on their walls and even though I know
the degradation of their lives I am moved my
Lord by their gestures of faith and devotion
bowing down with folded hands right down
to the ground and for those moments that
they are in front of their holy picture I see in
their eyes a little open to take in the deified
image and a little shut to internalize the vision of divinity I see a total giving up of

themselves to their God for that instant and I think of myself still trapped in the attitude of sophisticated worship of my church-going days of neat little genuflection and standing to attention with hands joined at the lower back never in front and lips firmly pursed in dignified solemnity and decorum never displaying piety or visible spirituality and I say to myself yes my Lord I will paint for these people their pantheon because I am certain that I will be giving them even for those few moments a oneness with your triune self in the form they have grown up to believe is yours and as for me I will hope still for the forgiveness of sins and the resurrection of the body and your promise of life everlasting

Memorare

Hail Mary and Hail Queen of Heaven and Hail Holy Mother of God and Hail our life and Hail our sweetness we have come to you this Wednesday to this Church of St. Michael for the Novena to Our Lady of Perpetual Succour all the way from our pavement yes Fatfatia's mother who I call Ma ever since that day of his going away and I have come to your feet as a last resort after we have been to the municipal hospitals and their doctors who have doled out their free medicines that

seem to have no effect still on the rasping
cough that my Ma has been having for the
past month from morning to night but more
at night as she sleeps beside me unable to get
her breath back at times with the severity and

stubbornness of the terrible thing inside her
which persists in its seemingly murderous
intent of strangling her to death and as I sit
up and watch her painful struggle to breathe
freely I feel out of breath myself in the empa-
thetic intensity of the moment so today we
come to you with hands outstretched and
palms heavenward in the suppliant attitude
that comes so easy to us of the pavement who
know how to run after rich Arab women in
their taxis and rich ladies who in their air-
conditioned limousines are still mothers with
a heart we know if only we sharpen our
moaning skills to melt the hardness of the
city in them O Mother of the whole world
though I have never begged yet on the street
I come with the most effective mendicant
pose that I can put on and which I am so fa-
miliar with dear Mother Mary look at me and
my Ma with our palms and eyes heavenward
O please look at us I pray and grant us our
petition at least a little relief to an old and
suffering mother that was gifted to me even

as once you were given by your son to his
disciple and to the whole world dear Mother
do you remember but what do I see around
me now but a sea of outstretched palms and
eyes rolled heavenward in attitudes that
would compete with the best on our pavement for the big notes from that Arab woman
in a taxi oh yes a thousand no two thousand
no three four five thousand pairs of upturned
palms and eyes competing with us for your
favour and I wonder who will you look at in
this entire congregation of mendicants no not
this congregation I know but billions all over
the world starting from here and Mount
Mary's and Mount Carmel and Vailankinni
and Fatima and Lourdes and Medjugore and
so many other corners of the world you have
one colossal basilica of mendicants oh yes I
can see our pavement extending across the
globe and I stop my pleading to ask myself if
it is right on my part to treat you like that
rich Arab woman in a taxi who drops her
currency into outstretched palms to get rid of

the nuisance or even out of genuine sympathy and drive away leaving the now rich beggar enjoying the success of making another sucker as they say I ask myself is it right my coming to you only in supplication because of my present need and is it right my flattering you with the name of Perpetual Succour only because we are perpetually supplicant tell me Mother Mary do you feel used when we hail you as Queen of Heaven only to slip smoothly into your mercy and your sweetness and our woe and into the mode of the poor banished children of eve moaning and weeping in this vale of tears tell us O Mary are you not worn down by the commitment he got you to make on the cross when he conferred the universal motherhood on you for all time for surely this burden was not part of Gabriel's message and your fiat or do you feel exploited after that precedent you set at Cana of Galilee because now even while I examine my conscience I hear the perpetual petitions of the people for cures from cancer and for

jobs for husbands and for husbands for spinster daughters and for the reformation of
drunken husbands and the return of prodigal
sons and of faithless wives and for success in
examinations and visas for emigrations and
for finding a good house or a lost necklace
and a safe journey and a good holiday and a
quick promotion and then follows the reeling
off of miraculous cures that have happened
and favours granted as a result of your inter-
cession and I wonder how many times can
you go to your Son and tell him that they
have no wine I wonder and is that why we
come to you with offerings of candles and
wax limbs and vows made as if to some pagan
goddess putting down conditions and twist-
ing your arm into listening expecting the su-
pernatural and the magical so we can yell
miracle miracle the Lord touched us in the
sight of the world I wonder as I close my eyes
and my mind goes back to the family rosary
that my mother would lead every evening before the evening meal yes full five decades of

aves and glory bes and the intended contem-
plation of the mysteries and ending with the
litany of your praises dear Mother and no we
did not ask for favours every day except on
occasions yes it was an honest devotion to
your divine motherhood recited aloud and
punctuated with instructions to the maid in
the kitchen and the occasional giggle and the
paternal boxing of ears but it was no demand
for favours at least in my mind so today dear
Mother Mary I close my eyes and fill myself
with that remembered attitude of pure devotion to you forgetting that I have come here
for my mother's cough as to a respiratory
specialist I come O Virgin in continuation of
that devotion I have for you for which the
tangible proof lies in the form of those broken beads of the rosary still in my pocket yes
I come much more ragged and completely
disconnected from the grace of the sacra-
ments O Mother I come with love for you
and for this mother bequeathed to me by a
friend all the while hoping not asking for

your kind favour O most gracious Virgin
Mary

Glossolalia

What in Heaven's name do I say to Your ruthless and eternal goodness who made me like I used to be and I am and I will be tomorrow please tell me how do I sing praises for my hurt feet and bruised hands and wounded heart and a conscience solidified by this pavement yes this Gabbatha of another kind and of all times yes this Gethsemane of the sinner not the Savior tell me how can I ask for the cup to be taken away and by what right can I make petition or raise a senseless

Alleluia to a broken ozone layer and to a
blankness above, below and all around and
inside of me a blankness that translates into
gibberish rich with emotion not meaning in
order to create a vocabulary of my private
reality in other words my madness and igno-
rance and anger and self-pity and remorse
and pride and distraction and good intention
and venality and a reaching up and Hope and
despair and confusion and nothingness nothingness and more nothingness shaped into
the vowels and consonants of the soul in
search of a tongue scanning the sounds of the
ether and the universe and all human experience to find those sibilant and labial and gut-
tural and palatal syllables that will envelope
the very particular nature of my feelings that
do not fit into any of those pious formulae
handed down to me on backs of holy pictures
and prayer books and missals or catechism
classes nor can even the sacred and secular
glossaries of the world provide me with the
mots juste to contain my fuzzy-edged feelings

today brought on by a sudden rush of dim
memories of fleeting frames and sequences
slowly dissolving into questions in my consciousness asking for answers and explana-
tions for people and places and happenings
like why my hands and feet were strapped to
a hospital bed and why the piercing screams
and shouts followed by jabs of needle in my
arm and a headlong fall into miles of cush-
ioned blackness with a thick syrupy warmth
traveling inside my veins filling me with a
fragile calmness picking out words which fly
into my hearing like bats on a moonlit night
seen only in highlight as they flap their meaning around my ears that prick up only a little
at the mention of my name as they tell each
other about me and about the fifth time I had
been admitted or was it the sixth and the sad
clicks of tongue and spurts of laughter and
questions with more questions about my
family who will not come to see me and what
about my friends all melted into thin air and
the bats get lost in the blackness of a cloudy

night so then how do I now bathed in the in-
candescence of the street lamps and drunken
eyeballs staring vacantly into the floating dust
particles speak to a god I do not see when all I
see again as in a jump-cut to the hospital bed
I see faces and I hear voices while a word here
and a word there flies into my consciousness
of NGOs and the sisters of the poor and of
good families on pavements till I get lost in a
limbo of unthinking and of sensing nothing
absolutely nothing blacker than sleep until a
slow rising to consciousness and the gentle
touch of a hand on my brow with accompa-
niments of voice and a face and the sensations of warm towels sponging my body and
my mind and my libido awakening some life
with its accompanying excitement and em-
barrassment and guilt because this warm
towel and palm of hand traveling pleasurably
over the seeming acres of skin and my rising
manhood is another kind of drug and that
face with the hand of the warm towel and
that voice coming back to me on this crowd-

ed pavement that face with no name racking my mind and memory to remember who she was but now I have sat down with the sign of the cross made some minutes ago as if it were the opening of a book of prayers that would just read itself for me to Him oh no the words I have are all wrong and too small to contain the meaning and the waves of feeling rising up in an old breast which need to break on some shore of cosmic attention without sinking into sands of indifference and forgetting so my fullness of experience does not meet with the hollowness of expression I eject the restless spirit overflowing with memories and hope and a heightened awareness of the moment into the unfathomed ocean of an unknown articulation and again that face and voice flash past with a remembered thinning of the clouds then leaving lacy mists which float across slow dissolves of consciousness of remorse and despair and self-flagellation and a giving up and once again and again that face of the gentle hand standing over me ask-

ing questions or speaking words of concern
and counsel and hope and affection expressed a little later with touch of hand now
not in duty but feeling on my fingers and
palm of hand before long over my face and
neck across my open chest and awakening
the me in me which I seemed to have lost for
long time like a Lazarus stepping out of a
tomb all coming back with other remembered scenes collapsing into a blurred vision
of forever and an eternal now oblivious of
where I am devoid of sensations and all
thought a thing with no form and no mind I
utter and hear the sound of my own resonating voice enveloping my soul with syllables of
praise and hope and thanksgiving and love
and worship on that Pentecostal pavement
for I don't know how long till when I open
my eyes I notice the drunken eyeballs staring
at me in silence

De Profundis

Did I have to wake up to the reality of grime and the gutters and even worse to the cruelty of my own thinking I ask you because that misty blanket of blankness and dreams and hallucination and that long death of consciousness was comfortable compared to the pain-inflicting hardness of thought and the jagged edges of memory and reason that I woke up to and wake up to every day like a Lazarus begging for a return to the tomb I hoped to crawl back into that limbo of unthinking that I floated in for so long before returning to the rude glare of the city and my own consciousness giving rise to shaken pride and self-flagellation and pity with apportioning of blame and the hurling of curses all the while flinching at the sight of

my own degradation and fall from that grace
of once upon a time into a pit made just for
me or so it seems a mire into which I sink
every time I think of my past and my future
of the stink of yesterday's gifts gone bad and
the hopelessness of things hoped for I struggle with the decisions on actions I must take
to retrace my steps towards redemption but
my feet get stuck my Lord in the convolutions of my brain gone soggy and my muscles
are paralyzed as if by a curare released by the
stubborn logic of my mind moving step by
step and back and forth and up and down the
thorny pathways and the spiraling staircases
of grudge and anxiety not being able in all
that rush of stale time to fix a gaze on my
trembling fingers and wobbly knees and the
way I feel as I amble without purpose from
one shelter to another when somewhere on
the torn screen of the Possible I see the im-
probable sequence for me of the Prodigal's
embrace and I slink away through the narrow
corridors of my ego into the mazes of a tor-

turous mind asking for punishment every
single day O my God why did I not stop the
slithering mind when she of the warm hands
and gentle voice came to me that afternoon
not in the nurse's white dress of the hospital
but in passionate red and painted lips like an
apparition from nowhere before me filling a
vacant present with the tangibility of flesh
and blood and concern right there on that
sea-face wall where penury sat with the jingle
of wealth and where lovers petted oblivious
of the public gaze and where the practiced
finger slid in and out of branded pockets she
stood unmindful of everyone else as she ca-
joled and counseled me to go back home to
family or at least to some respectable place
for which she would be willing to pay the rent
for a short time till I got myself a job she said
that anything and everything was possible for
a person as talented as I for she had gone
through my bag at the hospital and had seen
my drawings and the few things I had written
and she had looked into my eyes that now

and then sent out through the ground glass of
drug-induced blankness glimmers of meaning and depth such as she had not seen in any
other while she heard in the tone of my voice
and the refinement of my utterance which
though sparing in their economy of words
expressed thoughts and feelings that moved
her she said more than anybody else had ever
done she said and I ask you today why did
the Spirit of your enlightenment or at least
your mercy not break through the walls of
my pride and resentment to help me see
clearly even then to clasp the hand reaching
out to me my Lord and do I hear you now in
almost sorrowful reprimand inform me today
of the presence that day of the Spirit in dis-
guise right there before me sitting on the sea-
face wall against the grime of the city and the
petting couples and the crafty fingers in
pockets there in front of me she of the warm
hands and the gentle voice was the Dove and
the fiery tongue made visible and audible for
me but I saw and didn't notice yes I heard

and did not recognize the voice letting so
much redemption go waste Oh why do I have
to crouch through the dark labyrinths of yesterday's lost chances or is it necessary for me
to repent and chastise myself even more than
I already do for spurning your grace which I
desire but do not know how to receive Oh
why does the spirit not have the alacrity of
mind and the body to learn I ask why does
the spirit not respond as if by reflex to your
promptings without the need for conscious
effort of this thing called free will or is there a
way in which I can bury the flab of flesh and
fallible thought under the weight of my soul
O Lord it hurts to know that even in prayer I
slip into the mire of regret and infantile ques-
tioning and blaming *Eli Eli lama sabacthani*
uttered with an accusing finger pointed at
your divinity for my despondency and sinking spirit Lord I know that I have crawled out
somehow to this day to this pavement where
others too have come via other sloughs of
degradation and despair all the while moving

in and out of their own self-pity and self-
preservation and grit and challenge unmindful of right or wrong yes Lord I have moved
with them yet quite unlike the rest yes I have
lived with them in person but not conform-
ing in mind and spirit always befriended and
befriending the agents of sin and filth and
crime never condemning nor condemned by
them I linger at this station of solitude every-
day as I am doing now to know what con-
demnation is there for me from heaven and
for an eternal moment I see none O Lord for
if you did mark my iniquities I would never
have got even to this point of relative calm I
know I know that you are giving me chances
but to what end I ask my Lord because even
now I see in the occasional bursts of light that
come to me Lord I see that reconciliation
does not mean going back to the comfort of
acceptance and a return to the lifestyle of
clean sheets and conformity of family and a
friend circle but a turning back to a divinity
that now I cannot see but when O Lord when

Requiem

Yesterday I lit the pyre of the mother I borrowed from Fatfatia on the day of his dying and this morning while it was still dark I carried the earthen pot of her ashes to the Gateway of India and as the sun slowly peeped above the watery horizon like a bald head of a high priest coming up to bless the ritual I tilted that pot of nothingness into the ripples turned blood-red by the rising sun as if it had sprinkled the sacred kumkum over the waters and the silence for not a word came out of

my mouth and not a thought came into my
head for this one person in my whole life
whom I had taken responsibility for and
whom I looked after as best I could all

these years with the devotion of a son yes I
suffered her pain and choked with every fit of

coughing she had yes I held her close at
nights when the fits got worse even praying
to you God that I should be given a portion
of that pain because I knew I could bear it
more than that withering body but she bid
my worried face to put on a smile because she
had to go through it all she said to atone for
the wrong done to her son by people who did
not know they were doing anything wrong
like most people except the progeny of the
devil they do what they do not because they
are wicked but because they are driven by
blind passion or habit or the compulsions of
forces around them and because that wrong
has the power to wound the very fabric of
creation it is left for some men and women to
offer the gods their own hearts and bodies to
be pierced by swords of anguish and pain like
a surgeon's knife to heal that larger wound
and then steeped as I was in my traditional
catechism I could only crouch under the
strangely persuasive force of her personal
theology which was her comfort and I would

look unspeaking into her eyes till one day she
showed me soiled pictures of Mahatma Gan-
dhi and Christ on the Cross and the Mother
of Dolours and challenged me to explain to
her why these good people had to suffer so
much pain and even death which they did
with more than resignation a desire for as
much suffering as they would be given she
said because they had accepted a job from the
One who specially picked them for it and in
that one stroke it dawned on me that I had no
right to steal from her the consolation of her
self-canonization as God's professional mar-
tyr who would receive her payment from his
hands and so I watched every day her struggle for breath right up to yesterday when she
fell back into my arms like a pieta carved all
wrong O God I present this spirit to you
without so much as a sprinkling of water
and now my soul slides under the slime of
selfish thought to conjure up visions of my
own day of wrath and calamity not for a
moment able to come to terms with Ash

Wednesday's reminder on my forehead of my
own impermanence no it will not happen to
me at least not so soon I tell myself with finger on pulse to feel the fleshy metronome of
life's assurance my God will you take my life
before I discover after all these years the
meaning of me and of me and You and of
why it all had to be so and will you take me
away before the calming of the waters within
me because even now or rather especially
now with the fires turned to embers in my
being I feel the need to know or even sense
the purpose of it all because I truly cannot
reconcile myself to believing that I was created for some cosmic waste bin unlike the
mother-ash floating now in the Arabian Sea
beatified and sanctified in her own lifetime in
her own mind to go away in the end knowing
that it was all consummated and commend-
ing into your hands her spirit O God I am
nowhere there though I want to be yes I need
to feel your touch even here on the streets on
the pavements of a filthy city amid the daily

reenactment of Cain and Sodom and Gomor-
rah I am filled with the incompleteness of me
and yet somewhere inside my unknowing
there is a voice that tells me that You would
never leave a job incomplete even in the case
of one like me who deserved to be prema-
turely plucked and discarded and as I turn to
go back to our corner of the street struggling
with my resignation to Ma's passing away I
am faced with Ganga and Dondu and our
entire pavement community who had followed me silently and had watched my soli-
tary ritual they come to me one by one and
they throw their arms around me in a kind of
blending of so many griefs into one big wave
of feeling and I say to myself O God how infinitely beautiful this sacrament called Grief
is when it is shared because in that moment
the lines vanish between saint and sinner the
wealthy and the destitute and the cruel and
the kind-hearted so that for a moment at least
a death can buy redemption

Alleluia

Today I danced Lord and I am so happy because I do not usually dance no I don't do it because I cannot put one foot before another to a beat with any semblance of grace or beauty or vigor but then today I did it and I did it with your name on my lips and to think that it could all be traced to the day when Ganga was raped on the rocks while Fatfatia was in jail and we seethed in anger and the whole pavement ground their teeth and swore to tear those men in pieces if we found them but we didn't

and all the while the wretched girl hid herself
for shame after that terrible day crouching in
a corner weeping and moaning out loud and
wanting to kill herself day after day till her
loud moans gave way to silent tears and snif-
fles and then as the days moved into weeks
she moved about with a blank expression
which gradually gave way to one of calmness
with a hint of wonder as the weeks slipped
into months and the men looked at her face
and saw something new and even radiant in
her and they said she was turning into a saint
because of the way she endured her pain and
that that sainthood was now showing on her
face till the womenfolk whispered in their
husbands' ears the news that Ganga was
pregnant yes that woman was carrying the
bastard foetus of one of those rapists and that
she should be told to get rid of it before it was
too late the poor girl because how could she
bring up a child who would be pointed out by
everyone as one with no father and how
would she at her young age be burdened with

the responsibility of bringing up another
human being all by herself they said to one
another in well-meaning concern suggesting
that there were places that did these things
very cheap and there were also medicines and

herbs that a woman knew that could disinte-
grate the thing and nobody would know
about it at all and so one of the ladies went up
to Ganga and put the idea to her assuring her
of their support all the way and Ganga looked
serenely at the good lady and shook her head
saying softly that she would do nothing of the
kind and could not even think of it yes she
would keep it inside her where it belonged
and to the women who asked her how she
could bear to have the ejaculations of wicked
men growing inside her body she said that
everything inside her was hers now and a part
of her because she could feel a newness as if
she were being born again and not just making another human being she insisted softly it
was herself and nobody else but she and her
God who had a part in this thing thus reject-
ing firmly the suggestions of the women who
went away hurt and angry saying this is what
one got for being charitable and neighbourly
and that they never dreamed that Ganga was
a girl like that and could it be that she en-

joyed the thing when it happened and wanted to keep the memory of it with her and who knows the mind of young girls today and thus they left Ganga to herself telling each other that it was better to keep away from this wretch who chose to mother an illegitimate child and as I watched her in her loneliness not knowing what to say to her I looked to You for answers about right and wrong and about providence and justice but I got none perhaps because the answer was there right in front of me growing larger in the womb of this unfortunate girl now quite oblivious to everyone and yet at peace with herself as month followed month and then one day Dondu came over to me and said that she had said yes and I misunderstanding what he meant was aghast and asked him how she could agree to it at this stage when she was so big and Dondu said no it was not that at all but it was a yes that she said to him yes a yes she had said to his proposal of marriage yes yes yes and when the other men

heard it they shook his hand and praised him
for his courage and his big heart for doing
such a generous thing and he looked surprised at every one for thinking the way they
did for did they not know that it was she who
was generous and kind for accepting a simple
man like him while she was such a wonderful
person and a saint in his eyes and what a joy
it would be to look after Ganga and her baby
for life and how he would work extra hard to
earn some more money for her and for the
baby because she had finally said yes after
first saying no to his proposal for how could
she hand over to him the burden of looking
after two of them because the responsibility
and joy was hers alone till he looked into her
eyes and begged for a share in that joy and
she looked back into his for a long time and
with eyes filled with tears she softly said that
Fatfatia would approve yes he would and she
told her that she was hers if he wanted her
much to Dondu's great joy and when the
men had heard the story as it happened they

embraced that big hunk of simplicity one by one while I remember thinking how pleased You must be at this man and I going into one of my moods of introspection asked You why it was that Your grace was so accessible to the duffers of the world and if so why did You choose to give me the intellect that would ultimately damn me in Your eyes Oh why couldn't I be a simpleton like Dondu and not have to struggle the way I do with my spirit O God but today while I danced I stopped asking questions and I let my feet do the talking to You because it was so beautiful the way it happened when I accompanied Dondu and Ganga to their simple wedding ceremony and the next day she went into labour and delivered her baby girl and Dondu distributed pedas to the pavement beaming with joy saying he did not know whether the baby looked more like Ganga or him but that she was the most beautiful thing he had ever seen so he would like to call her Sundari if Ganga agreed and Sundari they called her when they brought her home and today being the fortieth day when Ganga could step out from the plastic cover that was her home she called whoever would come to the pavement altar of painted gods and began singing a *bhajan* to Lord Ganesh while everyone clapped their hands to the lively beat of the prayer *onetwothreefourfive onetwo onetwo* up to the point where Ganga forgot the words and the other women could not help her with them so the rest of us just continued clapping *onetwothreefourfive onetwo onetwo* Dondu louder than everyone else with a *tralala lalalala* to substitute for the lost words and then hands clapping he started moving his feet *onetwothreefourfive onetwo onetwo* and soon he was dancing a dance that became increasingly lively joined by his wife while we clapped and then he came over and dragged us into the center of the group and had us dancing with them hesitatingly at first very conscious of what a terrible dancer I was but before long I had lost myself in this prayer

feeling exhilarated at the vigor of it all as the
sweat streamed down my beard I lifted my
hands up to the clouds like the rest of them as
if asking for rain my eyes closed bumping
into the others and jumping higher and higher and faster and faster to the sound of clapping and panting and the sound of bare feet
on the pavement making a joyful noise unto
the heaven above and inside of us in that
endless moment of jolly worship expressing
Your divine praises from head to toe until
Dondu panting for breath with tears min-
gling with his sweat went inside his plastic
sheeted house to bring the little baby out and
place her on the pavement in front of the
gods to my inaudible Amen Alleluia

Dies Irae

There's a fire raging through my body O God and my mind feels like a furnace being fanned white hot by the bellows of strange contradictions now of remembering and forgetting of reason and dementia of helplessness and hope in between the throbbing pain that radiates up from a spot on my ankle from what started as a little sore three months ago and which has since festered and has grown nasty as a result of the dirt and neglect and the flies that cluster over it like miniature vultures around a carcass sending waves of excruciating pain like a volcanic lava through my veins burning my flesh and bringing my brain to a boil like a cauldron bubbling over with thoughts strangely unrelated to my suffering because between my silent weeping and wailing and gnashing of teeth I think with thankfulness of Kalia who applied an ointment from a tube that he had left over from years ago and of Gomti who prepared a poultice for me of some crushed leaves and powdered turmeric which she applied on the sore with her own incantations guaranteed by her to defeat this latest mischief of the devil and of Ganga's lavabo with warm water and boric acid powder and a paste made from turmeric and neem and the milk squeezed from her own still nursing breast and weeks later when none of it seemed to do any good and seeing that I could not even take more than a few steps on my own to walk to a clinic I found myself lifted off the ground by Dondu as if I were no more than an overgrown child despite my

protestations and when the doctor saw how
terrible the thing was he shook his head and
scolded Dondu and me for the sinful neglect
of it and with his head still shaking in disgust
at these illiterate street people he sprinkled a
dusting powder and tied a bandage to keep
the wound from being exposed to further in-
fection he said and sent us away muttering
under his breath but the stubborn thing continued to fester and grow bigger and more
painful and I have had to keep the dogs and
the flies away during the day with a rag tied
to a stick which I wave towards my foot
whenever I can muster up the energy to do so
while the pain gets to a level where I tell myself that it will be impossible for me to bear
any more and as if to spite me it gets even
worse till my whole body and not just my ankle is just one mass of painful flesh burning
with a high fever and mercifully at times I
just go blank in my head but for only a few
minutes and then I am back in the valley of
the burning lava and boiling cauldron and

lying there for days on end fingering those
broken beads and the bent little crucifix in
my pocket not asking You for healing or relief or for reasons why and I do not know
why my prayer to You is not the usual petition and self-pity and despair but just an unspoken but real sense of your presence
somewhere amid the pain which at times
looms so large that in that agonizing delirium
I imagine it is You who are this Great Pain
filling me and holding on to my being as if
You do not want to let go while I lie here in
my corner behind the makeshift curtain fash-
ioned by my pavement neighbors from an old
sari to keep the sun and the urchins from
peeping in on my unsightly discomfort pas-
sively letting things be and not asking for
help from the pavement or from You yet
dabbing as if with bold palette knife on the
cloudy canvas of my unconscious dim vi-
gnettes of the unlikely yet inspiring faithful-
ness of a mythical Job and the hallowed
wounds of a historical crown of thorns on the

one side and on the other I am scratching out
with furious strokes the intruding images of
the punishing hand and the day of judgment
and of wrath because try as I might I cannot
reconcile those images drawn for me by pulpit and home-spun catechesis of a God with a
cat-o-nine tails in His hand with those in my
consciousness though I must confess lying
here for months my mind has walked with
remorse and regret the paths of yesterday's
folly and transgression often causing anguish
enough to displace the burning lava and the
boiling cauldron in my body and yet in the
theology of my fevered brain which seems to
work overtime at times like these I am unable
to see my affliction as something flung by a
vengeful hand from above and I do not even
stop to think if I am creating for myself a divinity to fit my own limitations for have I not
grabbed with greed the pleasures of the mind
and flesh and have I not bought with money
and the coinage of conscience the many delights offered by circumstance yes did I not

glory in the triumphs of a pumped up ego
without stopping for a moment to think of
right or wrong and will I now not let today's
pain be no more than another place in the
continuity that is my life O God a purgation
after the feasting if you will or a necessary
incineration of the dross because as I close
my eyes and gnash my teeth in pain I look
into the depths of my personal purgatory
which today is revealed to me as a pus-filled
crater measuring a diameter of just one inch
on my foot so let it be yes let it be

Psalm

I don't know whether or not I have to thank you for this state I am in today O Lord the restful waters you have led me to for I do not even know how I feel right now walking in decent slippers across a disinfected floor and sleeping on clean sheets and a pillow every day because this body that had learned to soften the paving stones under my bones now aches over the cotton mattress which teases my muscles into a painful jelly and I am reminded of those days of detoxification in hospital only now it is a continuous

confinement for me in this home for the aged
where you have caused me to be brought for I
don't know what reason oh yes I know that I
was brought here from the hospital where I
was taken to be treated for the festering
wound on my leg yes that she of the warm
hands and gentle face had seen me one day
lying down with my leg stretched out as if I
had wanted my own foot to be as far away as
possible from the rest of me almost disown-
ing it like a sinful thing or like a Job disgusted
at his own sores and she quietly stood beside
my supine body on the pavement while I
looked at her face for quite some time before
I recognized her not just because of the angry
pain in my leg but because she was now in a
nun's white habit with her head and hair
veiled over but through which I could see
that she had grown considerably gray and she
bent down to shoo the flies that hovered over
my foot and she gently peeled the dirty cloth
that covered the wound to look closely at it
and then with a hint of almost personal pain

in her expression she said that the thing had festered and it had to be seen to or else it would turn gangrenous and we could not let that happen could we she asked under her breath as she hurried away without another word to me and returned later in a van that belonged to her institution and she made my pavement neighbours lift me into the vehicle and I was driven off to a hospital run by the order of nuns to which she belonged and she who I learnt was now called Sister Vimala arranged for me to have a mattress on the floor because there were no bed spaces available in that ward and as the treatment began and all through the days of lying down and doing nothing while the doctors moved from bed to bed placing diagnoses and prognoses like parts on a conveyor belt and the nurses did their follow-up assignments I knew that You O Lord had trapped me again into that monastery of my own reflection for what else could I do but think on You and me and everything that has taken place between us over

the years cursing the days when I was made
to walk through the valley of the shadow of
death for so long O Lord for so long I ask
why did you forsake me when I was in need
my God I know that I may have slipped or
taken a few wrong paths on the road pointed
out to me but did I not earn Your mercy for
all those years of my childhood and youth
when I gave to what I thought was your establishment on earth my self wearing out the
pews with my tender knees and filling the
nave with clouds of incense from the thuri-
fers I swung with so much altar-boy enthusi-
asm and all those beads I told and the sacra-
mentals that were sprinkled on and around
me I ask did they all count for nothing in the
face of my belief or at least my hope that they
were a shield against harm or hell and its
kingdom yes the same question marks that
have punctuated our relationship all these
years of my pavement pilgrimage come back
straightening out into exclamations of wonder at other times there in that position on

my back looking up at the ceiling and beyond
into a time which was never merely the present but a gigantic map spread out for my
consciousness to walk over focusing sometimes at what was under my feet and sometimes gazing at a distant past and future I
was grateful then for the moments of peace
and clarity of vision and the chances to distribute a portion of myself and my feelings to
those who needed them even there on the
pavement which is that great stream of human opportunity for both unbridled sin and
love and in those moments of relative calm I
see not the hard shapes of the reality around
me but the serene landscape and green pas-
tures of another reality inside made more visible and tangible today with the presence of
Sister Vimala who has now begun to stir in
me within the cubic acreage of my breast and
not skin as in the past a sensation of trembling as if a stringed instrument had just been
disturbed by a breeze for I was first conscious
of it as she took both my hands into hers to

pick me up off the mattress on the ground
and helped me take my first halting steps on
that slowly healing foot and she led me to the

waiting van that took me to the old people's
home where she said with a gentle firmness
that I should stay till my foot was completely
healed all the time displaying no expression
on her face but a nurse's sense of duty later
showing me to a room that I would have to
share with nine other old men and though I
was a little younger than some of them this
was the moment when it dawned on me that
at sixty-eight I was now to be counted among
the old yes You had brought me this far
without that realization because the pavement looked at one for what one was worth
to it by way of brute force or street smartness
or influence or sexuality or even a charming
vulnerability regardless of one's age so one
grew old only on the day one died having to
fend for oneself till the end like any other
able-bodied person and here I was an old
man among other old men as if I had left my
life behind and had to pick up another which
was in fact what I had to do I realized in time
when Sister Vimala came every day and gave

me a job to take up saying that the home
needed brightening up and it could use some
of my art all the while ignoring my protestations that I had lost it completely and that I
would never get my ability back now at this
age and she looked at me as if to an errant
child and said that she did not want to hear
any reference to age again and I noticed that
in spite of the gray hair and the wrinkles she
had a remarkable liveliness in her eyes and
then she smiled and fished out a few books
and pointed out to pictures that I could copy
or take as inspiration and here I am Lord
three paintings later still in this home where
every day I see wrinkled children challenge in
many cruel ways the compassion of persons
like Sister Vimala who I know now has lifted
her one time feelings for me into an offering
to you and I join my hands to the infinity that
pours it all out through those who are ready
to be channels

Silence

I feel cramps in my feet and a singing of crickets in my ears as I sit on this high bed with my feet barely touching the floor seeing a dark cosmic blue through closed eyelids give way to a black and then a spreading aquamarine with fleeting flashes of whitish-yellow as I turn my head ever so slightly and then tilt it upward towards heaven and You listening to the monotone of cricketsong or is it the sound of my nerve-ends swaying to the breeze and in the background the hooting of an owl persistent

against the sound of the ceiling fan and a car
horn and a few more hoots in answer becoming now a faint chorus lending a counter-
point to the sound of the nuns practicing in
the chapel in which I hear Sister Vimala's so-
prano as I notice that the cramps in my feet
have disappeared and I can feel the fan
breathe on my skin and in my hair as I lift my
hands a little with my palms upward and
holding them there I feel a rumbling in my
stomach building up to a discomfort and
some pain that moves downward slowly till I
know that I will now have to pass wind which
I do not resist and then I feel the relief not
just in my stomach but also in my legs and in
my head and I am conscious of the sound of a
mosquito hovering a little distance from me
with its hum louder at first than a passing
airplane then giving way to the sound of the
fan again in which I hear a sonic limp as it
were slowly being replaced by more distant
noises getting further and further away till I
feel that I can listen to a whispering on the

other side of the globe and beyond and soon I
am feeling the heave and fall of my chest very
slightly at first but getting larger and heavier
in my consciousness till the rhythm of it fills

me with a feeling as though I was nothing but
a blacksmith's bellows sucking the air in and
out and in and out till I become a balloon
which breath by breath loses its shape and
outer covering so that I feel as though I am
just so much air expanding and contracting
every time I inhale and exhale inside my
closed eyelids I am one with the atmosphere
and in that feeling of nothingness I sense a
warmth spreading inside my airy being like a
glow growing from the center of my nothingness outward and still further outward
beyond myself as if I did not exist and I feel
as if there were nothing under me nothing no
bed no floor nothing but me as a bundle of
nothing floating in the same place not side-
ways or up or down but stationary for I don't
know how long till imperceptibly at first and
then with a certainty that fills me with a little
insecurity I am in a cloud high above everything and I can see far below me the faint
outline of trees in a city dotted with lights
and I look upward and see a vast expanse of

light and slowly I bring my palms together and feel the skin of my left palm touch the skin of my right as if it were another and I sense the warmth now all concentrated between my two palms and the brilliance that was before me just a moment ago fades into gray as I slowly open my eyes to look around the dark room where I see the shapes of my other room-mates in their beds and then even before the shape of my body can return to my consciousness slowly Lord I lay my body down to sleep.